We're Going to Feed the Ducks

Margrit Cruickshank
Illustrated by Rosie Reeve

Gareth Stevens Publishing
A WORLD ALMANAC EDUCATION GROUP COMPANY

In memory of my mother,
an inveterate duck feeder ~ M. C.
For Jenny Reeve ~ R. R.

Please visit our web site at: www.garethstevens.com
For a free color catalog describing Gareth Stevens Publishing's
list of high-quality books and multimedia programs, call
1-800-542-2595 (USA) or 1-800-387-3178 (Canada).
Gareth Stevens Publishing's fax: (414) 332-3567.

Library of Congress Cataloging-in-Publication Data

Cruickshank, Margrit.
    We're going to feed the ducks / by Margrit Cruickshank; illustrated by
Rosie Reeve. — North American ed.
        p. cm.
    Summary: A girl and boy set out to take breadcrumbs to feed the ducks,
but they encounter some other hungry animals along the way.
    ISBN 0-8368-4027-5 (lib. bdg.)
    [1. Animal feeding—Fiction. 2. Ducks—Fiction. 3. Birds—Fiction.
4. Animals—Fiction.] I. Title: We are going to feed the ducks.
II. Reeve, Rosie, ill. III. Title.
PZ7.C88815We   2004
[E]—dc22   2003060986

This North American edition first published in 2004 by
Gareth Stevens Publishing
A World Almanac Education Group Company
330 West Olive Street, Suite 100
Milwaukee, Wisconsin 53212 USA

This U.S. edition copyright © 2004 by Gareth Stevens, Inc.
First published in Great Britain in 2003 by Frances Lincoln Limited,
4 Torriano Mews,Torriano Avenue, London NW5 2RZ, England.
We're Going to Feed the Ducks copyright © 2003 by Frances
Lincoln Limited. Text copyright © 2003 by Margrit Cruickshank.
Illustrations copyright © 2003 by Rosie Reeve.

Gareth Stevens editor: Dorothy L. Gibbs
Gareth Stevens art director: Tammy Gruenewald

Printed in the United States of America

1 2 3 4 5 6 7 8 9 08 07 06 05 04

We're going to feed the ducks!

Look! A friendly brown dog!
He looks hungry.

No! We're not going to feed
the friendly brown dog.
We're going to feed the ducks.

Look! TWO squirrels with bushy red tails!

No! We're not going to feed
the squirrels with bushy red tails.
We're going to feed the ducks.

Look! **Three** little baby sparrows!

No! We're not going to feed
the little baby sparrows.
We're going to feed the ducks.

Look! Four noisy pigeons!
Listen to them go *prruuu,*
prruuu, prruuuuu.

No! We're not going to feed
the noisy pigeons.
We're going to feed the ducks.

Look! **Five** squabbling seagulls!

No! We're not going to feed
the squabbling seagulls.
We're going to feed the ducks!

14

Oh, all right. Toss some breadcrumbs
to the **five** squabbling seagulls.
Here you are, seagulls!

Then we might as well give some
to the **four** noisy pigeons, too.
Here you are, pigeons!

And I suppose we can give a few crumbs
to the **three** little baby sparrows.
Here you are, sparrows!

Maybe the **two** squirrels with the
bushy red tails will eat out of my hands.
Here you are, squirrels!

Look! The friendly brown dog is begging!
I'll give him a slice of bread.

Now, we can feed the ducks!

Uh oh! Sorry, ducks.
The bread is all gone!

Don't worry. We'll get you some more.

We're going to feed the ducks!